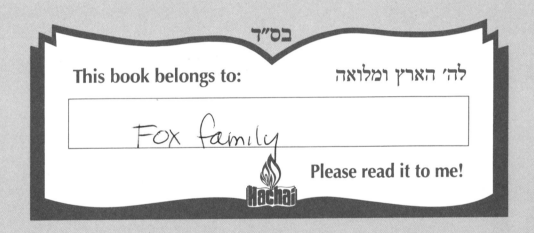

בס"ד

This book belongs to: לה׳ הארץ ומלואה

Fox family

Please read it to me!

The Sefer Torah Parade

by Tzivia Adler
illustrated by Ito Esther Perez

The Sefer Torah Parade

To Chana Wagh, who told me stories. T.A.
To my beloved daughters Odelia & Tamar I.E.P.

First Edition - Iyar 5765 / June 2005
Copyright © 2005 by **HACHAI PUBLISHING**
ALL RIGHTS RESERVED

ISBN: 1-929628-26-9
LCCN: 2005920512

HACHAI PUBLISHING
Brooklyn, New York
Tel: 718-633-0100 Fax: 718-633-0103
www.hachai.com info@hachai.com

Printed in China

Glossary

Aron Kodesh	Holy Ark
Bimah	Platform on which the Torah is read
Chuppah	Canopy
Mazel tov!	Congratulations!
Sefer Torah	Torah Scroll
Shabbos	Sabbath
Shul	Synagogue
Sofer	Scribe
Zeidy	Grandfather

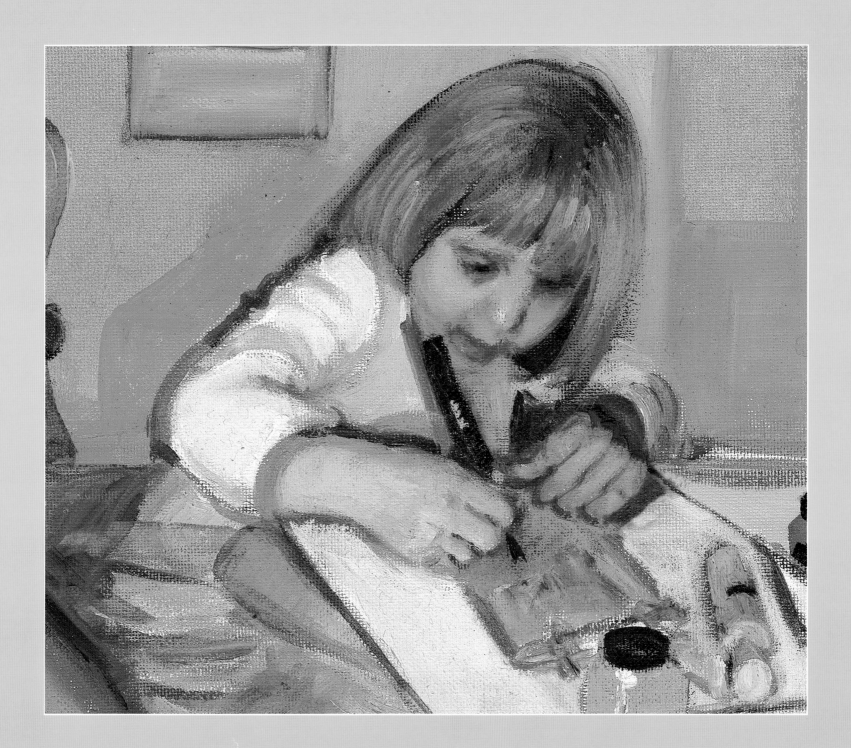

Today is a special day
because a new Sefer Torah
is almost finished.

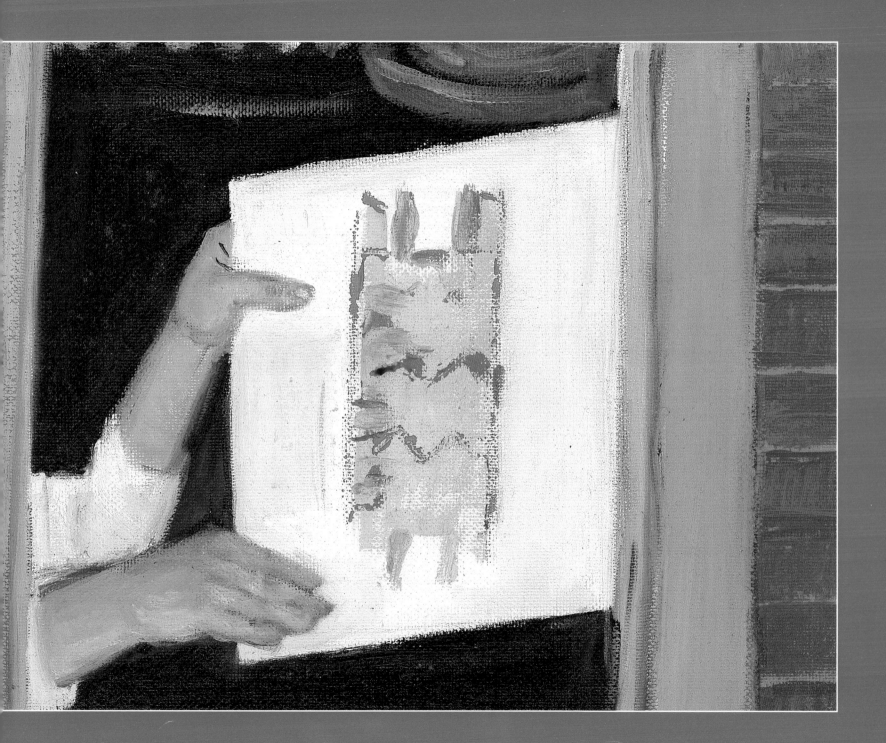

A sofer wrote the letters
very carefully. He used
soft parchment, a quill
pen and special black ink.
It took a long, long time.

Today, when the Torah is ready, we will take it to its new home in the shul.

We will march with it in a Torah parade!

Everyone is excited. We put on our Shabbos clothes and shoes. I can't wait to see what will happen next.

Look – people are taking turns to write the last few words. The rabbi writes one letter.

My zeidy writes one and so does my father. Finally, the Torah is finished! It is lifted up high for everyone to see.

Then the Torah is covered with a soft velvet coat.
Someone puts a shiny silver crown on top.

Now we can start the parade! A truck without a top waits outside. Gold cloth covers its sides.

A man sits in the back playing a small piano.
The music is loud and bouncy. Everyone claps.

One man gives torches with real fire to the
bigger boys.

Another man gives paper flags to little boys and girls like me. The flag says, "Be happy with the Torah!"

And here it comes! The rabbi is smiling and carrying the brand new Torah in his arms.

Four strong men carry four long poles with a velvet roof.
"That's called a chuppah," said Mommy.

What a parade!
A policeman walks ahead of the music truck.

He makes sure all the cars stop so it is safe for us to march down the street.

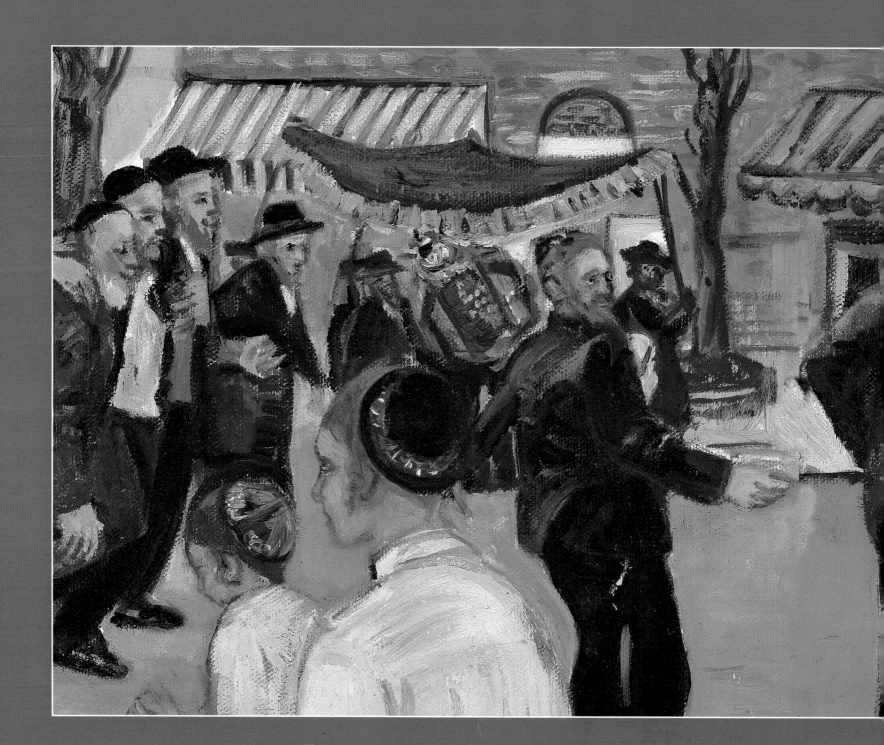

People come out of their houses to watch. Everyone starts to dance. Boys from a nearby school come, too. They sing and dance in our Torah parade.

My mommy pushes my stroller in case I get tired.
But I'm not tired at all. I dance and jump and wave
my flag! Mommy takes lots of pictures.

Now my feet are tired. I sit in my stroller. I still wave my flag and clap with the music.

When we are only
a block away from
the shul, a few men
run ahead.

They stand at the
door holding three
other Torahs.

"Welcome," they call
to the new Torah.
"Welcome home!"

The Torah comes close,
and I give it a big kiss.

The parade is over. The policeman goes away. The music stops playing. One man collects the torches and puts out the fire. I'm glad I get to keep my flag.

Everyone goes inside the shul to sing and dance around the bimah and to hear the rabbi read from the brand new Torah.

The Aron Kodesh looks like a little house.
The rabbi puts the Torah inside where it will
live from now on.

Mazel tov! It's time to celebrate!

I'm so happy that the Torah is home.